Magic Ballerina
Christmas in Enchantia

Welcome to the world of Enchantia!

I have always loved to dance. The captivating
music and wonderful stories of ballet are so
inspiring. So come with me and let's follow
Delphie on her magical adventures in
Enchantia, where the stories of dance will
take you on a very special journey.

Special thanks to
Linda Chapman and
Nellie Ryan

First published in hardback in Great Britain by HarperCollins *Children's Books* 2008
First published in paperback in Great Britain by HarperCollins *Children's Books* 2010
HarperCollins *Children's Books* is a division of HarperCollins *Publishers* Ltd,
77-85 Fulham Palace Road, Hammersmith, London W6 8JB

The HarperCollins website address is
www.harpercollins.co.uk

1

Text copyright © HarperCollins *Children's Books* 2008
Illustrations copyright © HarperCollins *Children's Books* 2008

MAGIC BALLERINA™ and the 'Magic Ballerina' logo are trade marks of
HarperCollins Publishers Ltd.

ISBN-13 978 0 00 734800 8

Printed and bound in England by
Clays Ltd, St Ives plc

Magic Ballerina™
Christmas in Enchantia

Darcey Bussell

HarperCollins *Children's Books*

To Phoebe and Zoe, as they are the inspiration
behind Magic Ballerina.

MERRY CHRISTMAS
SARA !

FROM LESIA
XO

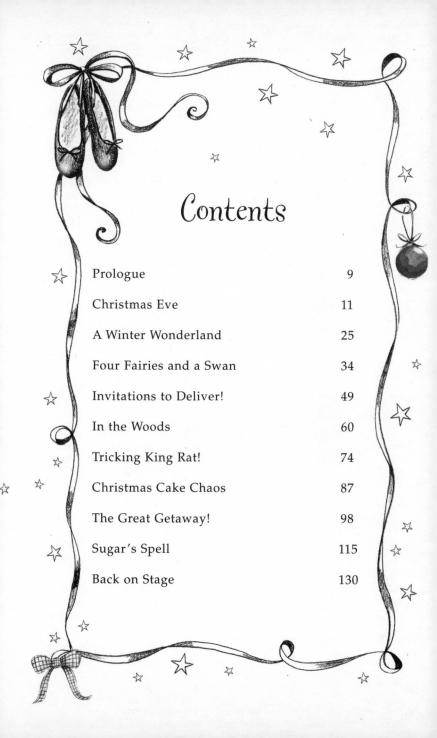

Contents

Prologue

*In the soft, pale light, the girl stood
with her head bent and her hands
held lightly in front of her.
There was a moment's silence and then
the first notes of the music began.
For as long as the girl could remember
music had seemed to tell her of
another world – a magical, exciting
world – that lay far, far away.
She always felt if she could just
close her eyes and lose herself,
then she would get there.
Maybe this time. As the music
swirled inside her, she swept
her arms above her head, rose on to
her toes and began to dance…*

Christmas Eve

Delphie Durand stood by the window, pointing first one foot forward and then the other. The clouds in the sky were grey and heavy as she looked out. People were hurrying along the street, their faces buried in their scarves, their gloved hands full of shopping bags.

Oh I hope it snows tonight, Delphie

thought longingly. She was nine and she hadn't once had a Christmas Day with snow.

"Delphie, do you want a mince pie?" her mum called from the kitchen.

Delphie ran through, leaping into the air on the way, to where her mum was washing up. A freshly baked batch of mince pies was cooling on a wire rack nearby.

"Well, would you like one?" her mum asked, nodding at them.

But Delphie's stomach felt full of fluttering butterflies. "Not now, thanks, Mum." Holding on to the back of a kitchen chair, she bent her knees, pulled her toe up against her leg and pointed it out to the side, her arm following gracefully.

She just couldn't seem to stand still that afternoon. She was too excited. Not only was it Christmas Eve but that night, Delphie's ballet school was doing a show at the town hall. Each class was going to be performing a dance they had been learning.

Delphie's group was going to be doing one from a ballet called *The Nutcracker*. They had been practising for weeks.

Mrs Durand checked her watch. "We should get going. We don't want to be late."

"I'll get my things," said Delphie eagerly.

She went up to her room and brushed her long dark hair. The nutcracker toy that she was going to be using in the dance was on her dressing table next to her red ballet shoes. Delphie picked him up and danced a few steps around the room, pretending to be Clara, the girl in the ballet who was given the nutcracker for Christmas.

Delphie smiled as she remembered another time when she had done the dance – and done it for real! For Delphie had an amazing

secret – her red ballet shoes were magic!
Sometimes they would start to glow and
sparkle and then they would whisk Delphie
off to a magical land called Enchantia where
all the characters from the different ballets
lived. That was where Delphie had met the
real Nutcracker and danced with him.

I wonder when I'll go to Enchantia again,
she thought.

"Delphie! Time to go!" her mum called.

"Coming!" Delphie grabbed her shoes,
ballet bag and the nutcracker toy and
hurried out of the room.

It was exciting to get to the town hall and
get changed in a proper dressing room with

everyone else from her class. The mirror in front of her even had lights all round it. Delphie had a space between her two best friends, Poppy and Lola.

Sukie Taylor, who didn't like Delphie much, was sitting on the other side of the room. "You're the last to get here," she said as Delphie sat down.

But Delphie ignored her. She wasn't going to let Sukie spoil her evening and although she may well have been the last to arrive, she knew she wasn't late.

"Hi, Delphie!" Poppy called over. She and Lola were fixing pink, blue and green ribbons in each other's hair. Delphie felt a flicker of longing. Her mum had only managed to get her plain white ones. She'd

seen her friends' ribbons at the dress
rehearsal and wished she'd had some the
same, particularly when Sukie had laughed
at her for being the only one with boring
white ones. Sukie's own ribbons were big,
wide and gold. Delphie thought they looked
a bit silly.

"We've got a present for you!" Lola
jumped up and handed her a small package
wrapped in Christmas paper. "Here!" she
smiled. "It's from both of us."

"Oh, thanks." Delphie felt awkward. She
hadn't realised they were getting each other
Christmas presents and hadn't brought
anything for her friends.

"Well, open it then!" Poppy urged.

Delphie unwrapped the paper. "Ribbons!

17

Just like yours!" she exclaimed as she pulled a set of green, pink and blue ribbons out of the paper.

"Now we can all be the same!" said Lola.

Just then their teacher, Madame Za-Za, poked her head into the dressing room. "Hurry up, girls."

Delphie started to get changed. They all

had to wear white leotards and knee-length white nightdresses. Over the tannoy system, Delphie could hear the sound of the audience coming into the town hall, talking and taking their seats. The orchestra was tuning up. A violin was playing a string of notes. Another musician blew a few deep notes on a tuba.

Poppy and Lola helped Delphie do her hair and then they started to warm up. Delphie bent and straightened her knees and thought about the dance ahead. It had been interesting watching the others at the dress rehearsal and seeing what they were good at. After the rehearsal, when she was practising at home, she had tried to skip as lightly as Poppy and to spin without wobbling like Lola and to lift her leg as high as Sukie, but the only problem was, the more she tried to be as good as the others at the different bits, the more her dancing just didn't feel right. *I hope it's going to be OK when I get on stage*, she thought nervously.

The tannoy crackled and there was an announcement. "Beginners to stage please. Beginners to stage."

Delphie's stomach clenched with excitement. "Good luck!" she said to Lola and Poppy and they all hugged. Even Sukie was looking anxious and as they got into line ready to go up to the stage, she caught Delphie's eye and gave her a nervous smile.

Delphie smiled back. "Good luck."

"Thanks," Sukie said, her nervousness making her nice for once. "You too, Delphie."

As they all hurried up the stairs on to the stage, they had to be very quiet. Standing out of the way of the stage hands, they watched the older girls before them go forward and get into their opening positions, waiting for the curtains to rise. Delphie didn't think she'd ever felt so nervous or excited. The lights in the auditorium went down and a hush fell. There was a moment's silence and then the orchestra started to play.

The curtains rose. The older girls were dancing a scene from *Cinderella*. One was a winter fairy, another was a summer fairy,

21

then there was a spring fairy and an
autumn fairy. It was the bit of the ballet
where all the fairies danced together. They
had to do lots of quick footwork including
dancing on their pointes and spinning
together perfectly in time. Delphie watched,

entranced, as they each took it in turns to do a short solo. She couldn't wait until she was old enough to have pointe shoes! One of the stage hands came over to them. "Time to get into your places, girls."

Delphie's class moved up to the curtains. Delphie had to come on alone from the entrance at the back of stage. She waited in the dark, out of sight of the others, hearing the loud applause as the older girls finished and curtsyed.

This is it, she thought, her heart thudding. *I'm about to go on!*

But just as her nerves almost started to get the better of her, her feet started to tingle. She glanced down at her shoes and stared. They were glowing! Surely she couldn't be about to go to Enchantia? Not at that very moment? Quickly she put down the nutcracker doll she was holding. Bright red, green and gold colours rushed around her as she was lifted up and swept away. Where would she land this time?

She couldn't wait to find out!

A Winterwonderland

Delphie spun down gently to the ground.
As the colours around her faded, she
stared in wonder. She was standing in
a town square covered in snow. Long
icicles hung from the roofs of the houses
and shops. A man was roasting chestnuts,
carol singers were singing and fairy lights
were twinkling in all the windows.

It looked wonderfully Christmassy.

Delphie waited for someone to come up and speak to her. The ballet shoes usually only took her to Enchantia when someone was in trouble. Who could need her help this time? She glanced around but everyone seemed to be very cheerful and happy. They were bustling around the stalls, buying food and presents and wishing each other a happy Christmas.

Delphie shivered and rubbed her arms before hurrying over to the chestnut seller's fire to warm up. The stall next to him was selling delicious-smelling gingerbread and tiny carved wooden figures of all the different characters from the ballets. Delphie spotted Cinderella, the swans from *Swan Lake*

and Clara holding a tiny nutcracker doll.
Delphie wished she had some money so she
could buy one each for Lola and Poppy. They
would love them!

"Delphie!"

Delphie looked round to see a familiar
fairy in a lilac tutu dancing towards her. It
was her friend the Sugar Plum Fairy. "Hi,
Sugar!" she called.

"Hi, Delphie." Sugar smiled and gave
Delphie a big hug. "I'm so glad you've
come!" Then she tapped Delphie's shoulder
with her wand. Delphie gasped as she
suddenly found herself wearing a long
red coat, black gloves and a black scarf.
"There, that will keep you warmer!" said
Sugar.

"Thank you!"
Delphie said
gratefully, pulling
the thick red coat
around her.
"So, what's
going on,
Sugar? Why
was I called?
Everyone
looks pretty
fine here."

"Yes, but they're not fine at the Royal
Palace," said Sugar lowering her voice. "It's
King Rat again. He's been trying to ruin
Christmas."

"Oh no." Delphie's heart sank. King Rat

was very mean and hated dancing. "What's
he done now?"

"I'll take you to the palace and the King
and Queen will tell you," Sugar said.
"Come on! There isn't a moment to lose!"

The fairy waved her wand and silver
sparkles swirled around them. Then Sugar
grabbed Delphie's hands and they spun
away through the air.

When they landed, Delphie found herself
in the ballroom of the Royal Palace. It
had been decorated with great swags of
red-berried holly, golden tinsel and red
ribbons and looked very festive. But the
King, Queen and Princess Aurelia didn't.

They were standing at one end of the hall, next to a table that was piled high with golden envelopes and were deep in worried discussion.

"I'm back!" Sugar called. "And Delphie's with me!"

The royal family looked round. Princess

Aurelia's face lit up. "Oh, Delphie! Thank goodness for that." She hurried over. "I'm so glad you're here! King Rat has ruined Christmas!"

"So I've heard. Sugar just told me," said Delphie. "But how can he have managed that?" she asked, curtsying to King Tristan and Queen Isabella.

"Come over here and we'll explain," said the King.

He led the way over to a group of comfy chairs near the fireplace and they all sat down. "King Rat hates Christmas," King Tristan said. "He likes the food and the presents, but he hates all the singing and dancing and he really can't stand people having a good time."

"But the rest of us all LOVE Christmas," said the Queen. "So this year I thought it would be a good idea to have a huge banquet on Christmas Eve."

"Tonight!" Delphie breathed.

"We were going to invite everyone in the land and have lots of food and dancing and presents," Princess Aurelia added.

"It sounds amazing!" said Delphie.

"It would have been," Princess Aurelia replied sadly. "But it's all gone wrong. The elves came to the palace to help us wrap the presents and when Mother went to check on them, they had all disappeared!"

The Queen nodded. "There was just a little red hat left on the bench with this." She reached into the pocket of her dress and handed a black card to Delphie.

Delphie looked at it. There was just a scrawling signature in gold:

King Rat

"He must have taken them!" Delphie gasped.

"That's what we think," said King Tristan. "And it's not only the elves who have gone either. The magic Christmas tree has been stolen as well."

"And we've been so worried about the elves and trying to work out how to rescue them, that we haven't had time to deliver the invitations for the banquet!" wailed Princess Aurelia. "Oh, Delphie, what are we going to do?"

Four Fairies and a Swan

Delphie's thoughts raced. *Kidnapped elves, a missing tree, invitations that hadn't been delivered…*

"Of course we *have* to rescue the elves, but first things first - we ought to try and get these invitations delivered," she said thoughtfully. "Then at least there can be a Christmas feast even if there aren't any presents and there isn't a tree."

"Delphie's right." Sugar nodded. "Presents and Christmas trees are lovely, but even without them we can have a really good time just dancing and having fun!"

"That's true," said Queen Isabella. "But how are we going to deliver the invitations in time? They have to go all over Enchantia."

"I could try to deliver them," suggested Sugar. "But even flying I won't be able to deliver *all* of them by this evening." She looked at the huge pile on the table.

Delphie frowned. "Isn't there anyone who could help you, Sugar?" She asked. "Other fairies maybe…" A picture of the stage back at home flashed into her mind. "What about the four fairies from

Cinderella?" she said. "Do they live in Enchantia? Couldn't they be brought in?"

"Of course!" said Sugar. "Why didn't I think of that myself? They're all friends of mine so I'm sure they'll help. That's a brilliant idea, Delphie. I'll summon them straightaway."

Delphie knew that to summon characters in Enchantia you had to perform some of the dance that they did in the ballet they were from. Sugar lifted her wand and the music from *Cinderella* began to play. She stood for a moment, her right leg turned out, her left leg crossed behind her, and her eyes looking down. As the music speeded up she suddenly stepped forward, full of lightness and energy. She spun around, her arms held above her head, then she jumped straight up and crossed her feet over before landing perfectly in balance. Dancing forward, she took three light leaps.

Delphie recognised the dance – it was that of the spring fairy and was full of light and life. Sugar spun and leaped, her feet crossing over and over until suddenly there was a flash of green light and a fairy appeared twirling round on her pointes, hands touching lightly above her head. She was wearing a knee length moss-green dress and had delicate gauzy wings. A circlet of leaves sat in her dark hair. She jumped gaily in the air too and did a side-stepping cat leap.

"Hello, Sugar!" she said giving the fairy
a big hug. "I was just wrapping some
Christmas presents for tomorrow. What do
you need me for?"

"I'll tell you when I've got the others here
too," said Sugar quickly. "Can you help me?
I was going to call the summer fairy next!"

The spring fairy nodded and she and
Sugar began to dance. The music was much
slower this time, giving a feeling of long
lazy summer days. They stepped together
across the floor with long graceful steps,
their arms at shoulder-height, stopping
with one foot crossed behind the other,
their right arms above their heads and their
left arms to the side. In one smooth
movement they knelt down, sweeping their

right arms towards the floor and their other arms behind them. Then they straightened up and moved across the floor with slow, controlled spins, both perfectly in time with each other. Suddenly there was a flash of golden light and a fairy dressed in a golden-yellow dress with a golden circlet in her hair appeared.

In no time at all the autumn and winter fairies were also summoned – the winter fairy wearing a dress of a delicate icy blue and the autumn, a dress of yellows and oranges. They all hugged each other in greeting.

"So what do you want us for, Sugar?" the winter fairy asked curiously.

"To give you these," Sugar said, handing them each a golden invitation. "And to ask for your help." Sugar began to explain.

As soon as the four fairies heard what was the matter, they offered to help.

"It would be so lovely to have a Christmas banquet for everyone," said the winter fairy wistfully.

"Of course we'll give out the other invitations," said the spring fairy.

"Oh thank you!" said the Queen.

"The poor elves," said the summer fairy, looking worried. "I wish we could help them. But our magic won't work in King Rat's castle."

"Mine doesn't either," said Sugar.

"Well, we'll all keep thinking of a way to rescue the elves," Delphie promised. "But if you could just deliver the invitations that would be a really good start."

"Which of us should go where?" asked the autumn fairy.

Sugar magicked up a map of Enchantia and opened it out on the floor before tapping it with her wand. The map quickly divided itself into five sections, each one labelled with a different fairy's name.

"Brilliant!" said the winter fairy. "Let's get going!"

Delphie looked at the piles of invitations on the table and realised a problem. "The envelopes are very big," she said. "How are you going to carry them all?"

The winter fairy smiled and pirouetted. "Easy. We will use our fairy magic of course!" She touched her wand to the envelopes on the table and they immediately shrank down to postage stamp size.

Delphie gasped. "Now they're easy to carry," the winter fairy smiled, starting to put the envelopes into her bag. "We can make them bigger when we deliver them!"

"That's brilliant," said Princess Aurelia and Delphie agreed.

"Who's going to deliver King Rat's invitation?" asked the King. "His castle is in the east so I suppose that means it's you," he said looking at the map and then looking at the autumn fairy.

She looked worried and scared. "Oh."

"We don't *have* to invite King Rat, do we?" Princess Aurelia said. "He's the one who's trying to spoil Christmas for everyone."

"Oh, but we do have to invite him,

43

Aurelia," said the Queen, standing firm.
"That's what we decided – that everyone
had to at least be asked. I'm sure he won't
come, but if we give an invitation to
everyone else we *have* to give one to him.
It's the spirit of Christmas *and* the spirit of
Enchantia."

"Bad things happen when you don't
invite people," sighed the King. "We made
that mistake at your christening."

"But he's so mean!" protested Princess
Aurelia.

"I… I don't want to go to his castle," said
the autumn fairy in a small voice. "He
scares me."

Delphie knew that feeling only too well,
but she didn't like seeing the autumn fairy

looking so unhappy. "Don't worry." She glanced at Sugar. "Sugar, could you use your magic to take me to his castle and I'll deliver him his invitation? Maybe when I'm there I'll also be able to have a look around and see if I can find the elves?"

"I could use my magic," said Sugar. "But I can only take you as far as the woods outside his castle and then what would you do? You can't just go walking up to his home and put an invitation through the door. You've stopped King Rat's plans so many times in the past he would be bound to tell his guards to catch you and throw you in his dungeons!"

Delphie realised that Sugar had a point. But she couldn't let the poor autumn fairy go.

"I know!" said Princess Aurelia suddenly. "If you really have to do it, what about Sabrina?"

"Of course," said Delphie, thinking of the leader of the swans from *Swan Lake*.

"She's here in the castle," Princess Aurelia went on. "We invited her and the other swans for Christmas. She flew you away from King Rat's castle before, didn't she? So maybe she would fly you back there now?"

Delphie nodded eagerly. But now Princess Aurelia was starting to speak again.

"You could throw the invitation through the letterbox," she said. "Then have a look for the elves, but escape before the guards could get you."

"Do you think she would do it?" asked Delphie eagerly. It had been an amazing experience flying on the giant swan's back before and it would be a brilliant way to get to the castle.

"I'm sure she will," said Princess Aurelia. "I'll go and ask her!"

She ran off and a few minutes later came back with a beautiful swan beside her. "Hello, Delphie," Sabrina said softly as Delphie ran over. "Princess Aurelia has told me you need my help."

"Yes, please!" said Delphie. "I'm going to deliver King Rat's invitation so none of the fairies have to do it. Will you take me there?"

"Of course I will," said the giant swan.

"I'll come too," said Sugar. "We can deliver my invitations first."

"Then what are we waiting for?" said Delphie, with a shiver of excitement. "Let's go!"

Invitations to Deliver!

The four season fairies set off and Delphie and Sugar climbed on to Sabrina's soft white back. Calling goodbye to the royal family, Sabrina, Delphie and Sugar swooped out of the palace and across the courtyard.

It was a perfect day for flying. The sky was blue, the winter sun was shining and a

blanket of snow covered the fields beneath
them. The branches of the trees sparkled
with frost and everything
in the land seemed
to glitter and shine.
It was amazing to
soar through the
sky above it all.

Whenever they
saw a house or a
castle beneath them,
Sugar would swoop down
and pop an invitation through the letterbox.

While she was delivering an invitation to
Prince Charming's castle, Delphie couldn't
help but notice there seemed to be an awful
lot of big, prickly cactus below them. She

hadn't seen them on her other trips to Enchantia, but before she could ask Sabrina about it, Sugar was flying back up to them. "There's just one invitation left – King Rat's!"

"I guess we'd better go and deliver it then," said Delphie, thinking about King Rat's dark and smelly castle and not feeling quite as brave as she had done in the Royal Palace.

Sabrina sensed her nervousness. "We'll fly down quickly," she said reassuringly to Delphie. "I'll head straight for the guards on the door and hopefully they'll jump out of the way. Then you can just drop the invitation down beside them."

"OK," said Delphie trying to be brave. "I want to look out for the elves too though."

They flew over the forest towards King

Rat's castle, and when they got to the edge
of the trees Sabrina swooped down. The
castle was to their right and Delphie could
see two of King Rat's fierce mouse guards
standing by the huge front door. There
were three big sleighs near them. Delphie
wrinkled her nose at the smell of old
rubbish that lingered in the air.

"I'll have to stay here," said Sugar. "I
won't be able to fly if I go out of the forest
and into his grounds."

"Here goes then!" said Sabrina. "Hang on
tight, Delphie!"

Delphie clutched Sabrina's feathers. The
swan burst out of the trees, beating her
huge wings as hard as she could.

As they swept past the big window

towards the front door, Delphie looked in,
wondering if there would be any sign of the
elves. There wasn't. There was just a massive
Christmas tree with a few bits of old
bedraggled tinsel slung carelessly over it.

Sabrina flew straight towards the guards
as if she was going to attack them. They
yelled and threw themselves on the ground.

"Now, Delphie!" Sabrina cried as she
flew over the two mice.

Delphie chucked down the invitation. It
landed on the doorstep. One invitation
safely delivered!

As Sabrina soared upwards, the guards
scrambled to their feet, yelling and shaking
their fists. "Get the bows and arrows!" one
shouted to the other.

"If they're getting bows and arrows we'll have to go," said Sabrina quickly to Delphie.

"But what about the elves?" Delphie said. "I wanted to have a look for them."

"It's too risky," said Sabrina.

Delphie gave in. "OK." She didn't want Sabrina to be hurt.

"You did it!" cried Sugar as they reached the forest again and circled back to meet her. "You delivered the invitation."

"We did," Delphie said breathing out a sigh of relief. "But we didn't see any sign of the elves and then the mice were threatening to get out their bows and arrows."

"Oh dear, well I guess we'd better get back to the palace," said Sugar. "We can try and think of a plan to rescue them when we're there."

* 🌀 * ☆ 🌀 * ☆ 🌀 * ☆ 🌀 *

Back at the palace, the friends sat down in front of a roaring log fire with the royal family and told them what had happened. The King ordered hot chocolate with marshmallows sprinkled on top and iced gingerbread biscuits for everyone. Delphie sat in a comfy armchair with Sabrina beside her and sipped her drink.

"Well, the other fairies should be back soon from delivering the invitations," said the Queen. "So at least the banquet will go ahead now."

"But we still have to rescue the elves, Mother," said Princess Aurelia. "We can't possibly have a party knowing the elves are King Rat's prisoners. We've got to free them!"

"Of course we do," said the Queen. "But how?" She looked at Delphie.

But Delphie didn't know.

"And there's the missing Christmas tree too," said the King. "It's not going to be much of a banquet without it."

"Couldn't you just put up another tree?" said Delphie

The King sighed. "I wish we could. But we won't be able to find one. King Rat was so determined to ruin Christmas for everyone that he turned all the Christmas trees left in the land into cactus plants."

Delphie stared. So that was why she had seen so many of them.

"Our tree didn't turn into a cactus," said Princess Aurelia. "It just disappeared. It's a special Christmas tree that has belonged to our family for hundreds of years. It grows in an enormous pot in the grounds and the gardeners bring it in every year. As midnight strikes on Christmas Eve it gives a special present to everyone who lives in the household where it is. It's always something they need."

"This year when the gardeners went to bring the tree in they found that it had gone," said the Queen. "We were very upset, but we thought we would get

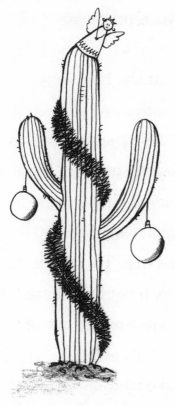

another one so at least people would have a Christmas tree to look at…"

"And that was when we found out that King Rat had cast a spell to turn all the Christmas trees into cactus plants," said the King.

"I wish we knew where our lovely tree was," said Princess Aurelia sadly.

"I think I might know," said Delphie, remembering the magnificent tree in King Rat's castle. "I think King Rat's got it!"

"What?" said the King, Queen and Princess Aurelia.

Delphie explained what she had seen through the window.

"He must have taken it so that he and his guards could all get presents from it," said Princess Aurelia. "We have to get it back!"

Delphie looked at Sugar. King Rat had the elves *and* the palace's tree. There was only one thing for it. "We have to go back to King Rat's castle and this time go inside," she said, standing up.

Sugar nodded. "I'll take us to the edge of the woods outside the castle and then we can try and think of a plan!"

"Good idea," said Delphie. "We simply can't let him ruin Christmas!"

In the Woods

Delphie and Sugar landed among the trees near King Rat's castle, their feet crunching on the frosty snow. Three large sleighs were still standing outside the doors and the two guards were still there. Delphie's heart beat fast. The mice looked even scarier now she was on the ground and not on Sabrina's back. Their teeth were sharp and pointed and long swords hung from their leather belts. Their black eyes darted around suspiciously.

"How are we going to get past?" she said in a low voice. "We can't just walk up there and you can't use magic to get us inside."

"And what are we going to do if we *do* get in?" said Sugar. "How will we ever find the elves and escape with the Christmas tree without being captured?"

Delphie wracked her brains. Suddenly she heard the sound of light footsteps in the snow behind her. She jumped in fright and swung round, expecting to see a guard.

But it was a deer with a spotted coat and large dark eyes. Her ears twitched as she stared at Delphie and Sugar.

Sugar held out her hand and the deer came closer. "Please will you help me?" she said timidly.

Delphie only felt a flicker of surprise that the deer could talk. Most of the animals in Enchantia seemed to be able to speak out loud. "What's the matter?" she asked.

"My fawn is stuck. We can't free him. I heard you talking and came to see if you might be help."

"Of course we'll help," said Sugar, looking at Delphie who nodded. Getting into King Rat's castle could wait.

The deer bounded away, stopping a little way down the snowy track. "He's this way! With the rest of my herd."

Delphie and Sugar followed, their feet

sinking into the snow. Luckily Delphie's magic ballet shoes always kept her feet warm in Enchantia, even when it was icy cold. They followed the deer to a clearing and stopped.

Delphie caught her breath. A large herd of deer were standing around a small fawn. He was tangled in a bramble bush. Its long thorny branches wrapped round his legs. A stag was using his antlers to try and push the brambles away, but they were caught too tightly. The fawn's eyes were wide and frightened as he bucked and struggled, trying to get out, but all the time making himself more and more caught up.

"I've found some help!" bleated his mother. The other deer looked round as Delphie

hurried forward. "We'll get you free," she said to the baby.

She crouched down near the fawn and began to untangle the branches. The thorns scratched and tore at her fingers but she took no notice, gently pushing the fawn away as he tried to nuzzle her. Sugar came and helped. With two of them working it didn't take long and soon the brambles were untangled and the fawn was free. He bounded away from the bush in delight.

"Thank you!" he said, putting his head down and kicking his heels up in the air. "Thank you very much!"

His mother made a bleating noise and nuzzled him over and over again before looking gratefully at the girls. A stag, who seemed to be the fawn's father, walked forward and bowed his head. "Thank you very for freeing my son," he said in a deep voice.

"That's OK," said Delphie. "I'm just glad we could help."

"What are you doing here in the woods?" the stag asked.

"We've come to try and rescue some elves and a Christmas tree from King Rat," said Sugar.

The stag nodded. "Ah, that explains it. Three nights ago we heard the sound of sleighs and saw them pulling sacks towards the castle by King Rat's mice. There seemed to be something inside the sacks, struggling and shouting. I hope you can rescue them."

"Thanks," said Delphie, turning to wave as she and Sugar hurried back through the woods.

Now that they had rescued the fawn, Delphie's thoughts returned to how they were going to get into the castle. *There's no way of simply sneaking past*, she thought, looking at the guards on the door. *We'll have to get them to let us in. But how?* She frowned. Maybe if they were delivering something, something that King Rat wanted…

Quickly an idea formed in her head. "Sugar!" she hissed. "King Rat eats Christmas food, doesn't he?"

"Of course," said Sugar. "The food and the presents are the only bits of Christmas he likes!"

Delphie grinned. "OK then. I think I might have an idea. I'm going to need you to do some magic!"

A minute later, Sugar was dancing through the snow. She waved her wand and there was a flash of silver light. A wooden sledge appeared with a massive towering pile of freshly baked mince pies. Sugar pointed her wand again and a second sledge appeared. This one was carrying an enormous iced Christmas cake with three tiers and a robin on top. It was almost as big as Delphie!

"Perfect!" said Delphie clapping her hands together as the delicious smell of mince pies and cake surrounded them.

"So we're going to pretend we're delivering food from the town bakery, are we?" said Sugar, waving her wand and magicking herself up a cloak and scarf too.

"That's the idea." Delphie nodded. "Pull

up your scarf and put your hood up, then hopefully the guards won't recognise us. We'll be able to get inside the castle and go and explore!"

"It's a great idea!" said Sugar. "But we must be careful." She took hold of the rope on the sledge of mince pies.

Delphie picked up the other rope and they set off out of the forest.

As the two mice saw them trudging across the snow with the sledges they started to point and nudge each other. They drew their swords. Delphie took a deep breath and marched on. *I'm not scared, I'm not scared*, she told herself, burying her face deep in her scarf and hoping they wouldn't recognise her.

"Halt!" the taller of the two guards shouted. He was skinny and bony with a wart at the end of his nose. "Who are you? And what do you want?"

Delphie cleared her throat. "We're from

the Enchantia bakery. Christmas delivery
for King Rat."

The other guard, a smaller fatter mouse,
edged forward smelling the mince pies.
"Hey, Sarge, these smell good. Do you
think King Rat will let us have some?"

The tall bony guard's nose twitched, but
he continued glaring suspiciously at
Delphie. "We haven't been told about any
delivery," he said, waving his sword
menacingly. "We'd have been told!"

"The message can't have got through
to you," said Sugar quickly. "Please let
us in!"

The fat mouse nodded eagerly. His
whiskers were millimetres away from the
tray of mince pies. "Yeah, go on, Sarge!"

The tall mouse hesitated, but then shook his head. "No!"

A window above the heads flew open. "I can smell something! What can I smell?" snarled a voice. They looked up and saw King Rat looking out! His crown was gleaming on his greasy black fur. His red eyes glittered as he stared at Delphie and Sugar.

Despite the cold, Delphie could feel sweat prickling down her back. What if he guessed it was them?

"A cake! Mince Pies!" King Rat said as if he couldn't believe his eyes. "What's going on?"

"You ordered them, your highness," Sugar said desperately.

"I didn't. It's a trick!" King Rat's eyes gleamed and his voice snapped out. "Guards! Get them!"

Tricking King Rat!

As the guards leaped towards Delphie and Sugar, Delphie gasped. "It isn't a trick!" she cried. "It's… it's… it's a mistake!"

The fat guard had grabbed Sugar and the thin guard had grabbed Delphie. He was so close she could see his pointed yellow teeth. "We… we must have come to the wrong castle," Delphie said, the words tumbling out of her. "Yes, yes," she said nodding furiously as if just remembering. "It was the Royal Palace we were supposed to go to. How silly of us!" She looked at Sugar. "These mince pies and this cake weren't meant for King Rat. They were meant for Queen Isabella and her family. We're so sorry to bother you," she said to King Rat. "It was the Queen who said she wanted the biggest most tasty Christmas cake ever with the thickest softest icing *and* the most freshly baked biggest mince pies. We'll take them all away and drop them off at the palace…"

"Wait!" King Rat snapped as Delphie tried to pull away from the guard. "You're saying that that cake and those mince pies are supposed to go to the Royal Palace?"

Delphie nodded. "Yes, we had *really* strict instructions that no one else was to have any."

"Guards! Let them in!" King Rat bellowed. "I'm going to have those mince pies and that cake for myself!"

Delphie acted shocked. "But... but you can't!"

"Says who?" said King Rat. "Just think of how cross this will make Queen Isabella and her family. Another way for me to ruin their Christmas. Ha! Bring them in! I'm coming downstairs!" And, with an evil laugh, he slammed the window shut.

Delphie saw the astonishment on Sugar's face and started to speak. "Oh well, if King

Rat really wants them I guess there's nothing we can do," she sighed trying to hide her smile.

"Yes," said Sugar, as the guards nodded. "I suppose we'll just *have* to take them inside."

The mice guards opened the door and ushered them through.

King Rat's hall was a huge room with stone walls and floor. Faded tapestries covered the walls. Many doors led off the hall and a stone staircase spiraled downstairs. The Christmas tree was by one of the windows, but there was nothing else Christmassy in the room at all.

King Rat came hurrying in. He was rubbing his paws together in glee. "All this food for me!"

A longing, whimpering squeak left the fat mouse guard.

"Oh all right!" snapped King Rat. "I suppose I'll never eat it all by myself anyway. You guards can have some too because I am so nice and kind and generous. What am I?" he said, grabbing the mouse by its fur.

"Nice and kind and generous, Sire!" gasped the mouse.

King Rat nodded. "Exactly. Now take the mince pies through to the kitchen. We'll eat them straightaway and have the Christmas cake tomorrow."

"You!" he snapped to the tall guard. "Go and get a trolley to put it on and tell the others." He swiped a mince pie off the top

of the plate as the fat mouse began to pull
the sledge with the mince pies past him.
Stuffing it all into his mouth in one go, a
look of pleasure lit up his eyes as he
chewed. "Delicious!" he said, spraying
crumbs everywhere, helping himself to
another as he followed the mouse.

The smell of the warm mince pies wafted
through the castle and by the time the tall
mouse had heaved the cake off the sledge

and on to a trolley the guards had come pouring into the hall from all over the castle. Elbowing each other out of the way and standing on each other's paws, they piled into the kitchen, their whiskers twitching greedily. Shouts came through the doorway.

"That's mine! Get off!"

"Hey, you've got five! Give me one!"

"I've only had two!"

The arguing grew louder. Delphie glanced around. There was no one about. "Now's our chance!" she hissed to Sugar. "Let's see if we can find where King Rat is keeping the elves while everyone is busy!"

Quickly, they hurried around the room

on tiptoe, listening at each of the doors. When they got to a staircase leading downwards, Sugar grabbed Delphie's arm. "Listen! I can hear voices!"

Delphie could too. A faint sound was coming up the stairs. She could hear what sounded like hammering on a door. "I bet that's them!"

She and Sugar ran lightly down the spiral staircase. At the bottom was a wooden door. Now she could hear the voices more clearly.

"Let us out!"

"It's Christmas. We have to get out and wrap presents!"

"Stop keeping us prisoner like this!"

Delphie swung round to Sugar. "It *is* them!"

"And look!" Sugar pointed. "The guards ran off to get to the mince pies so quickly that the key is still in the lock!"

She turned the key and threw the door open. Behind it were about twenty-five small elves with red and white woolly hats, striped stockings, green tunics and turned-up shoes. Their ears stuck out of their hats and their faces were cross as they all shouted. But as they looked at Sugar and Delphie, their crossness was replaced by looks of astonishment and they stopped shouting. All except a few elves at the back who couldn't see out of the door, but they were quickly shushed.

"Sugar!" exclaimed one of the elves at the front. "What are you doing here?"

"Delphie and I have come to rescue you!" Sugar said. "Delphie's the girl with the magic ballet shoes. We tricked our way into the castle, hoping we could set you free and think of a way to get the magic Christmas tree back. King Rat's got it in his hall!"

"He's horrible!" said the elf. "He shut us down here with nothing but bread crusts to eat and water to drink!"

"And to think we should be in the palace wrapping presents!" said the elf beside him.

"Well, now you can get back there," said Delphie. "Though how we're going to get you all back I don't know." She looked at Sugar hopefully.

But Sugar shook her head. "My magic isn't strong enough to take all the elves back, even from the woods."

"Well, first things first. Let's just get you out of here before the guards finish the mince pies and come back," said Delphie.

But she hadn't realised just how quickly King Rat's guards would finish them all up. Just then there was the sound of voices from the top of the stairs. "How many mince pies did *you* eat?" There was a loud burp. "I ate seven."

"I had eight!" said another voice.

"I suppose we'd better go and check on those annoying elves," said a third voice.

"Yeah. We can tell them all about the lovely mince pies we've been eating," said another voice. "And then get them some more bread and water! Ha, ha ha."

There was the sound of sniggering and then footsteps on the stairs.

Delphie's stomach felt as if it had just dropped to the floor. The guards were coming down! It was too late to escape. They were trapped!

Christmas Cake Chaos!

The guards' footsteps echoed on the stairs.

"What are we going to do?" Sugar said in panic.

The elves whispered frantically among themselves.

Delphie's thoughts raced. There was only one thing for it. "Shussh!" she said quickly to the elves. They kept quiet and looked at her. "There are more of us than there are of them. And they don't know the door is unlocked," she told them. "We can take them by surprise. On the count of three start to run up the stairs. If we all charge together maybe we'll be able to knock the guards over and get out of the castle."

"But what are we going to do once we've done that?" said one elf.

"We'll worry about that then!" said Delphie. "Let's just get out first!"

Now Delphie could hear the guards more clearly. They were puffing and panting. "Are you ready?" she hissed. The elves and Sugar all nodded. "One, two…"

"My tummy hurts," one of the guards was moaning.

"And mine," said another.

Delphie took a deep breath. "… THREE!"

The elves poured out of the room and charged up the stairs, carrying Delphie and Sugar along with them. Within a couple of seconds they were upon the mice guards.

"What the…" the first guard staggered backwards and bumped down on to his bottom.

The second flung his arms out. "Stop!" he shouted.

But the elves ignored him, ducking under his arms and spinning him round like a top.

The third mouse was grabbed by the elves and carried up the stairs above their heads. Cheering and hollering, the elves burst out into the hall.

The other guards were walking slowly around, their tummies fat with mince pies. They stared for a moment in astonishment and then pulled out their swords but the small, nimble elves easily ducked and dodged around them. Grabbing the waddling mice by the arms, they twirled them round until they fell over, sprawling on to the ground. Delphie saw one elf duck through a mouse's legs, sending him flying. Another two elves grabbed a couple of the tapestries from the walls and flung them over a group of mice who were charging towards them. The mice fell down, rolling over and over in the tapestries until just their heads were poking out and they looked like colourful sausage rolls!

Delphie and Sugar hung back by the trolley with the Christmas cake, not knowing where to run or what to do.

"Quick, get the Christmas tree!" cried one elf.

A group of about ten elves charged towards it, grabbed it, tipped it over and picked it up. They swung it round knocking over five mice who had just been getting to their feet. Holding it like a battering ram they charged at another group. The mice jumped out of the way, tumbling over on the floor. An elf near the entrance threw the door open and the group carrying the tree raced towards it.

"What is going on?"

It was King Rat!

As he stood in the kitchen doorway, crumbs smeared down his front, he took in the scene. His eyes narrowed in fury as he saw the group of elves racing towards the door and raised his hands.

"He's going to magic the doors shut!"
Sugar cried, seeing exactly what was just
about to happen.

Delphie grabbed the nearest thing – the
cake trolley – and ran with it a few paces
before giving it a huge shove. King Rat
had his back to her and didn't see it
coming. As he opened his mouth to utter a
spell, the trolley collided into the back of
his legs.

"Argh!" he yelled, arms flailing as he
was knocked off his feet. He turned a
somersault in the air and came down,
landing slap bang in the middle of the
cake!

Delphie's hands flew to her mouth and
she giggled.

With a roar, King Rat poked his head out. Icing hung from his whiskers. "Why, you... you..." he spluttered in rage.

Delphie grabbed Sugar's arm. "Come on! Let's get out of here!"

And quickly they raced across the hall, dodging around the fallen mice.

The elves with the tree were charging outside whilst the others streamed out behind them. Delphie and Sugar ran through the door, Delphie quickly turning to check there were no elves left behind. Then she grabbed the key from the inside, slammed the door shut and locked the door from the outside.

But there wasn't a moment to lose. Already the mice were starting to tug open the windows and she could hear King Rat shrieking. "Go round the back!"

"How are we going to get everyone back to the palace?" she cried to Sugar.

"I don't know," wailed Sugar. "If only we could use the sleighs, but we've got no way of pulling them!"

Delphie was suddenly aware of the elves crying out in astonishment. She looked round and saw a herd of deer cantering out of the forest. It was the group that she had helped earlier and the father stag was in the lead. "We'll help you!" he cried.

In the twinkling of an eye, the elves with their nimble fingers hitched eight strong deer to each sleigh. The tree was put on one sleigh and the elves and Delphie and Sugar climbed on to the other two.

Delphie looked round to see the mice jumping down from the windows and running round the side of the castle. "Quick!" she shrieked.

The deer surged forward and the sleighs glided across the snow, with the elves,

Delphie and Sugar hanging on. As they gathered speed, Delphie glanced behind. King Rat, dripping icing sugar everywhere, was standing furiously in one of the windows. He raised his hands to make his magic but he was too late. The deer swept the sleighs into the forest and away!

The Great Getaway!

The sleighs raced smoothly across the snow, the deer galloping, the elves hanging off the sides. Three of the elves were sitting astride the tree trunk as if it were a horse. Sugar waved her wand and a thick fur rug appeared over her and Delphie's knees for them to snuggle under. Delphie's face was

tingling with the cold as white crystals of
snow flew up in the air around them. She
could hardly believe they had managed to
escape with the elves *and* the tree. She
hugged her arms around herself. It was
beginning to look as if King Rat hadn't
ruined Christmas in Enchantia after all!

They raced through the forest, across the
fields and all the way to the Royal Palace,
arriving as the clock struck five o'clock. The

guards spotted them coming and by the time the sleighs had reached the palace, the golden gates had been flung open. The reindeer galloped inside, coming to a halt inside the courtyard.

The King, the Queen and Princess Aurelia came hurrying out to meet them with Sabrina.

"Oh my goodness!" cried the Queen as the elves tumbled off the sleighs.

"You did it!" said the King.

"Well done!" said Sabrina proudly.

"Now we can finish wrapping the presents!" said one of the elves.

"Hooray!" the other elves all cheered and started running into the palace. "Back to work!"

"So what happened?" Princess Aurelia demanded as Delphie and Sugar climbed off the sleigh.

As they began to undo the harness on the reindeer, they explained. Everyone chuckled when they heard how King Rat had fallen into the cake.

"Serves him right!" said Princess Aurelia.

Delphie grinned as she remembered how funny King Rat had looked covered in icing. "At least we got away. And we couldn't have done it without you," she said, turning to the magnificent stag. "Thank you!"

The stag tossed his head. "One good turn always deserves another. Now we must return to our home. Happy Christmas to everyone here!" He and the other deer turned and bounded back to join the others in the forest.

"Happy Christmas!" everyone called.

Princess Aurelia hugged Delphie. "So the invitations have been delivered, the elves are wrapping the presents. All we need to do now is decorate the Christmas tree and get changed for the banquet!"

"I'll go and check on the food," said the Queen.

"And I need to talk to the musicians," said the King.

"And I should go and join the other swans," said Sabrina.

Delphie grinned at Sugar and Princess Aurelia. "Then it looks like we'll be doing the decorating!"

In no time at all, Princess Aurelia had called the gardeners and they carefully put the tree in the corner of the ballroom. Two metal chests of Christmas tree decorations were carried out and music began to play. Delphie recognised the piece from *The Nutcracker*. She felt her feet tingle. The music was making her want to dance!

Sugar grabbed Delphie's hands and twirled her round. "Come on! Let's decorate the tree!"

"We have to dance while we do it," said Princess Aurelia, jumping in the air and crossing her feet over before landing lightly. "Or the tree's magic won't work and no one will get any presents."

Quickly, Princess Aurelia ran over to the chest with tiny steps in perfect time to the music and took out a big glittering red bauble. She lifted it gracefully with both hands and spun round on her toes, holding it high in the air. Pointing her right toe she danced forward two steps, spun on one leg, holding the toe of the lifted foot close to her knees, and then danced forward another two steps before placing the bauble on the tree. She looked light and elegant and beautiful. Delphie sighed wistfully.

As Sugar began to join in, Delphie watched carefully and tried to imitate her movements. Like Princess Aurelia, Sugar spun on her toes but she swept the bauble up more dramatically, holding it in one hand and stretching the other arm out to the side before jumping forward. Delphie wasn't sure who to copy.

"What's the matter?" Sugar said, seeing her standing still.

"You and Princess Aurelia are both doing different things," Delphie replied.

Sugar smiled. "Every dancer dances

differently. You have to make the dance your own."

"How?" said Delphie.

"By listening to the music and showing how it makes you feel." Sugar squeezed Delphie's hand. "Try it."

Delphie waited a few bars until the music reached the point where it seemed to be telling her to start and then she let it guide her, skimming across the ground with tiny steps, jumping into the air with arms outstretched and head held high, spinning and turning and balancing.

"Beautiful!" Sugar whispered as she danced past and Delphie glowed.

Delphie always loved decorating the Christmas tree back home but this was even

more special. They hung sparkling baubles
and long twisted icicles, golden wire stars
and carved wooden robins. Sugar flew into
the air and attached the biggest star to the
top of the tree and then finally, when the

chests were empty, she touched the tree
with her wand and magic white fairy lights
appeared on every branch. The music faded
and the three friends were left looking at
the tree.

"It's perfect!" Delphie breathed.

"Just beautiful!" Princess Aurelia agreed.

"Christmas wouldn't be Christmas
without a tree," said Sugar. "I wish there
was a way of making all the others turn
back from cactus plants so everyone who
wanted one could have one!"

Delphie nodded. It would be lovely for
all of the guests to see the magic Christmas
tree but it would be even nicer if they all
had their own at home. But there didn't
seem any way to solve *that* problem!

"We should go and get changed now!" said Princess Aurelia as the clock struck half past six. "Come on!"

It was fun getting ready. Sugar magicked up a beautiful red dress for Delphie. It was embroidered with gold thread and had a knee-length red net skirt scattered with tiny golden stars, matching her ballet shoes perfectly!

Princess Aurelia put on a gold dress, a tiara decorated with rubies and golden ballet shoes. Sugar wore her usual lilac tutu but she had magicked herself up a sparkling silver cloak that fell from her shoulders and floated behind her.

They hurried downstairs as they heard
the carriages start to arrive. The King and
Queen were already there and Sabrina and
the other swans had joined them too. It was
dark and frosty outside and the guests

hurried in, beaming as the warmth of the palace enveloped them. On either side of the entrance way there were two pots each with a cactus plant in. The Queen had done her best to make them look Christmassy by decorating them with bits of tinsel but they still looked quite strange with their spiky leaves.

Delphie was delighted to see people she knew arriving – the four season fairies were followed by the Nutcracker. He could either look like a wooden toy or a handsome prince and this time he was a handsome prince dressed all in white and gold. Delphie was delighted to see him. "Hello, Nutcracker!" she said running over.

He picked her up and swirled her round.

"It's good to see you again, Delphie!" he said before placing her lightly down and striding over to Sugar. He held out his hand and she took it. Carefully he lifted his arm and she turned beneath it, stopping just beside him as he kissed her on the cheek.

More people arrived. There was Cinderella and Prince Charming with Cinderella's fairy godmother. Even Cinderella's ugly sisters were there, arguing with each other as to which one of them looked the most

beautiful as they stomped into the ballroom.
All of the guests stopped to hug Delphie,
Princess Aurelia and Sugar.

"*Croak!*" Delphie jumped and looked
round. Priscilla the giant toad who Sugar
had once transformed to look like a
beautiful princess was hopping into the
palace through the door. "*Croak!*"

Delphie grinned. Priscilla was always
grumpy. But suddenly the smile died from
her face.

"Out of my way!" a familiar voice could
be heard snarling outside. "I want some
food and a present! And no, the mice aren't
coming. I've told them they've got to stay
behind and guard my castle!"

A figure in a black cape and long black

boots was striding through the doors, red eyes gleaming, whiskers curled, golden crown on his head.

It was King Rat!

Sugar's Spell

Sugar hid behind a pillar and Delphie quickly joined her. After their escapade at the castle, the last thing she wanted was for King Rat to see her.

Oh, why did he have to come, Delphie thought, her heart sinking. *He's going to ruin everything!*

King Rat certainly looked as if that was

his plan. He shoved the summer fairy out
of the way, making her fall over. Then he
swept off his cloak, knocking the Fairy
Godmother's tiara and throwing it on the
floor for a servant to pick up. "Where's the
food?" he demanded, glaring round with
his beady eyes.

"The food will be served shortly, your
highness," said one of the servants nervously.
"Would… would you like to go to the
ballroom first? There's dancing there."

"Dancing!" spat King Rat. "Pah! I don't
want to see any dancing! In fact," his eyes
narrowed thoughtfully. "Maybe I've got a
way to stop it. If I could just make the
music stop… hmmm…" He reached into
his pocket.

"Sugar!" Delphie said in alarm. "He's going to try and spoil the banquet!"

"Don't worry," said Sugar bravely. "My magic is stronger than his in the palace."

"Yes, if I just cast a spell…" King Rat went on.

Sugar danced out behind him, music tinkling around her, her wand outstretched. *"From your castle you have come to grumble and eat…"* She danced towards him, spinning round and round, covering the ground between them quickly.

"You!" King Rat snarled. "Why you…."

Sugar hastily spoke above him. *"But here all that you say will be kind and sweet!"*

And before King Rat knew what she was doing Sugar had tapped him on the head

with her wand. There was a lilac flash. For
a moment King Rat scowled and blinked,
but then the corners of his lips twitched,
pulling upwards into a crooked smile.

"Good evening, Sugar Plum Fairy. How
lovely it is to see you," he said. His eyes
darted around as if horrified at what he

was saying, but he couldn't seem to stop. "Everywhere is looking so beautiful. I particularly cannot wait to see the dancing." He whimpered as his smile stretched even wider.

"Excellent," said Sugar. "There's going to be a lot of it."

King Rat glared at her but his mouth kept smiling. "How perfectly… perfectly… *wonderful!*" he burst out, almost with a snarl.

Delphie couldn't stop herself from giggling. King Rat turned and saw her so she grinned. "Do you like Christmas trees, King Rat?"

He gritted his teeth. "I… I *love* them!"

"It's such a shame that all the Christmas

trees have been turned to cactus plants then, isn't it?" said Delphie.

"Oh yes, I really wish…" King Rat clamped his hands over his mouth in horror as if he realised what he was going to say but he couldn't stop the words from bursting out. "I really wish they would all just turn back into Christmas trees!"

Ping!

The Fairy Godmother to one side of him had instantly waved her wand in the air. "Your wish is granted, King Rat!" she said, with a beaming smile. "And I've made sure they can't ever be changed again – isn't that splendid?"

Jumping up and down in rage, King Rat turned and stomped away into the night as everyone burst out laughing.

Inside the ballroom the music started up.

"The dancing's about to start!" said Sugar. "Come on!"

As everyone hurried into the ballroom, Sugar and the Nutcracker started off the dancing. They stopped in the middle of the floor while the King and Queen sat down on their thrones beside the band and everyone else stood at the side of the room.

The lights dimmed apart from two spotlights on Sugar and the prince and at the same time the King motioned to the musicians to begin. Beautiful music flooded the air. Sugar slowly lifted her head and her arms, rising on to her pointes. She looked at the prince, slowly extending an

arm towards him before pausing for a
moment on her pointes. Then she began to
spin across the floor towards him, turning
rapidly. As she reached him he swept her
up into the air, holding her high above
himself, making her look as light as

thistledown, before sweeping her down
and following her as she danced away.

Delphie clasped her hands. Sugar and
the Prince danced perfectly without the
slightest wobble or mistake, their eyes
hardly leaving each other's faces.

The dance got faster and suddenly the
music changed to a waltz. It seemed to be
the moment everyone was waiting for. They
all swept on to the dance floor. Princess
Aurelia grabbed Delphie's hands and
pulled her among the crowd. They spun
around in time to the music. Delphie
laughed out loud and then felt the
nutcracker put his hands lightly on her
waist. He swung her up into the air.
Delphie held her arms out at the sides and

lifted her chin. She felt as if she was flying like a bird. He carried her forward and then placed her lightly down. Grinning at him, she pirouetted round and then danced away.

Everyone was dancing. Even the elves could be seen standing around the outside of the room twirling each other round. Delphie had never had such fun! In the corner the fairy lights on the Christmas tree were twinkling brightly, and through a set of doors she could see a room full of Christmas presents, beautifully wrapped by the elves, just waiting for

everyone to take them home. Through
another set of doors she could see a huge
room with an enormous feast laid out. There
was every type of Christmas food that she
could imagine – a huge great turkey, piles of
roast potatoes, great bowls of cranberry jelly,
Christmas cakes, mince pies and a stack of
little Christmas puddings with silver pieces
stuck inside and holly on the top.

Sugar grabbed her hands. "Are you
enjoying Christmas Eve in Enchantia?"

"Oh yes," breathed Delphie. "I am!"

They ate and talked and laughed and danced.
The evening flew by until it was midnight
and the palace clock was chiming out.

"Come quick!" said Sugar, pulling
Delphie closer to the Christmas tree.

On the twelfth stroke there was a bright
golden flash of light and a heap of presents
appeared around the tree's base.

Princess Aurelia crouched down, quickly
looking at the labels. "Delphie! Here's a
present for you. I was hoping there would
be." She picked up a small parcel and ran
over with it.

"It's for me?" Delphie said in astonishment.

Aurelia nodded. "Go on! Open it! It's
after midnight so it's Christmas Day now. I
want to see what you've got. The tree always
gives you a present you really need."

Heart beating fast, Delphie began to open
the wrapping paper as the King and Queen

handed out the other presents to the servants.

As the last layer of tissue paper fell off, Delphie gasped. There were two wooden ballet figures inside. Each of them was a figurine of Clara holding the nutcracker doll. A smile slowly spread across her face.

"Two figures the same? That's strange," said Princess Aurelia in surprise. "Why didn't the tree give you two different figures?"

"Because these are what I needed," said Delphie softly, looking at the beautifully carved figures. "They are perfect!"

Her feet began to tingle. Looking down she saw that her ballet shoes were glowing and sparkling. "I'm going home!"

"Goodbye, Delphie, see you next time!" cried Sugar.

"Happy Christmas!" called Princess Aurelia.

"Happy Christmas everyone!" Delphie cried looking round at the happy, festive room. The next second she was whisked away in a swirl of red and gold light. She whirled round and round, her fingers tightly clutching the wooden figures. She knew *just* what she was going to do with them.

As she spun down, the haze of colours cleared. She was back in the town hall and the opening bars of the music for her dance were swelling out. The performance was about to begin!

Back on Stage

Delphie hastily put down the wooden figures and picked up the nutcracker doll. She took a deep breath. It was lucky that time in the real world always seemed to stand still whist she was in Enchantia. Her adventures were still whirling in her head, but she knew she had to concentrate on dancing now. *I've got to be Clara*, she thought, *dancing with her nutcracker.*

She took another deep breath and then it was time for her entrance. She ran on to the stage with the rest of her class. It was dark in the auditorium where the audience was sitting and she could only see the first few rows of faces.

She ran forward with tiny steps, aware of all the others from her class doing the same thing around her. She noticed Poppy moving so lightly that she almost looked as if she was floating across the floor. Delphie felt herself stiffen. Sugar's words floated into her mind: *Make the dance your own.*

Delphie blocked out her friends and what they were doing. She listened instead to the music and focused on the nutcracker. She raised the toy, drew her right leg up against her left and stretched it out behind her.

Then she spun into a pirouette, skipped forward a few steps and leaped into two cat jumps just as they had been taught. Lifting the nutcracker high up she turned round with him, her whole body glowing and light.

When the dance ended and Delphie was holding the final pose, she blinked as she suddenly became aware of the town hall, the stage and her friends around her. During the dance she had forgotten her nerves and her doubts, lost in a world of her own. She heard the audience applauding loudly. Delphie and the others curtsyed before running off the stage as they had been told.

Madame Za-Za was waiting in the wings. "That was wonderful, girls!" she whispered. She caught Delphie's eye. "Magical," she said, with a smile.

Poppy and Lola ran over to Delphie and grabbed her hands. "Wasn't that brilliant?" said Lola her eyes glowing.

"It was fantastic!" gasped Delphie.

The stage manager started motioning to them to go back to the dressing room.

Delphie remembered something. Quickly
running back to where she had left the
wooden figures, she picked them up, then
she followed the others down the stairs.
The dressing room was full of excited
chatter and girls hugging.

Delphie joined in as they all talked about
what they had done and what it had been
like. The girls had to stay in their costumes
for the final bows at the end of the show. It
was wonderful to go back on to the stage
and curtsy in front of the audience again.
The people in the town hall clapped so
much that they had to curtsy five times
before the curtain came down!

After they had all got changed, it was
finally time to go home. Delphie took the

two beautiful wooden figures out of her
bag where she had been keeping them safe.
"Poppy! Lola! I've got something for you
for Christmas. I'm… I'm sorry they're not
wrapped."

As her friends took the figures and
looked at them, smiles broke out on their
faces. "Wow!" said Poppy. "These are
beautiful. Thank you, Delphie!"

"They're gorgeous," said Lola. "Where did you get them from?"

Delphie hid her smile. "Oh, just a stall in a market I know," she answered.

"Time to go, girls!" Madame Za-Za called. "Your parents are waiting outside."

They hurried out of the dressing room and up the stairs. As they ran into the small back street behind the town hall where their parents were waiting, Delphie gasped. Snow was falling, the flakes caught in the soft amber glow of the street lights. "Oh, wow!" she gasped, looking around at the white world.

Her parents hurried over and her dad enveloped her in a hug. "You were great, Delphie."

"Thanks," Delphie smiled. "I can't believe it's snowing!"

"I know," her mum replied. "It's wonderful. It looks like we are going to have a white Christmas this year after all."

"We should get home now," Delphie's dad said. "You don't want to be in bed late tonight or you'll be too tired to enjoy Christmas Day tomorrow."

"Bye!" Poppy and Lola called, as their parents started to urge them away too. "Happy Christmas, Delphie!"

Delphie waved. "Happy Christmas!"

Happiness filled her. Everything was perfect. She'd had an adventure in Enchantia, danced on stage, made her two best friends really happy, tomorrow was

Christmas Day *and* it was snowing. What could be better?

She felt so joyful that she just had to dance. She pirouetted round, her arms outstretched to the sides, her face turned up to the sky.

"Come on, Delphie," her mum said, looking round and laughing.

Delphie jumped into the air. *Happy Christmas*, she thought, picturing her friends in Enchantia. Then she danced after her parents, snowflakes glittering in her dark hair.

Meet other girls in Enchantia over the page...

Hi, I'm Rosa. I've always loved dancing! Madame
Za-Za tells me to slow down and concentrate on
what I'm doing, but dancing is just so exciting.
Delphie gave me the precious red ballet shoes and,
before I knew it, I was in Enchantia meeting all the
ballet characters. Nutmeg (Sugar's sister) and I
have been on lots of adventures: rescuing an
enchanted princess, finding stolen treasure and
thwarting the Wicked Fairy at every turn.

Hair colour: Blonde

Eye colour: Blue

Likes: Olivia my best friend, making my mum happy

Dislikes: Making mistakes or losing my temper

Favourite ballet: Swan Lake

Best friend in Enchantia: Nutmeg

Read all my Magic Ballerina adventures...

Hi, my name's Holly and I love ballet more than anything. Dancing makes me think of my mum because she's a professional dancer. I love the emotions and stories in ballet, sometimes I get so carried away I forget where I am! Luckily I'm always in the best places: dancing at Madame Za-Za's or in Enchantia! The White Cat and I have done so much there: protecting Cinderella from an evil magician, reuniting Beauty and the Beast, and even making things right in the Land of Sweets!

Hair colour: Dark brown

Eye colour: Green

Likes: Expressing myself through dancing

Dislikes: Feeling left out

Favourite ballet: Sleeping Beauty (particularly the Rose Adagio dance)

Best friend in Enchantia: The White Cat

Read all my Magic Ballerina adventures...

Darcey Bussell

Buy more great Magic Ballerina books direct from HarperCollins at 10% off recommended retail price.
FREE postage and packing in the UK.

Delphie and the Magic Ballet Shoes	ISBN 978 0 00 728607 2
Delphie and the Magic Spell	ISBN 978 0 00 728608 9
Delphie and the Masked Ball	ISBN 978 0 00 728610 2
Delphie and the Glass Slippers	ISBN 978 0 00 728617 1
Delphie and the Fairy Godmother	ISBN 978 0 00 728611 9
Delphie and the Birthday Show	ISBN 978 0 00 728612 6
Rosa and the Secret Princess	ISBN 978 0 00 730029 7
Rosa and the Golden Bird	ISBN 978 0 00 730030 3
Rosa and the Magic Moonstone	ISBN 978 0 00 730031 0
Rosa and the Special Prize	ISBN 978 0 00 730032 7
Rosa and the Magic Dream	ISBN 978 0 00 730033 4
Rosa and the Three Wishes	ISBN 978 0 00 730034 1

All priced at £3.99